THE BIRDCAGE HEART & OTHER STRANGE TALES

THE BIRDCAGE HEART & OTHER STRANGE TALES

PETER M. BALL

A Brain Jar Press Book
www.brainjarpress.com

ISBN 9780648176114 (Ebook)
ISBN 9780648176138 (Print)

*For Kate Eltham and Rob Hoge, who made so many things happen
behind the scenes*

CONTENTS

THE LAST GREAT HOUSE OF ISLA TORTUGA

She enters my name as Tobias Truman. I watch her ink the delicate curve of the capitals, the ostrich-feather quill dancing as she writes. My name is entered below Mr. Drummond's, his below the Captain; two of the three marked with the swooping X that denotes the status of a paying guest, a true patron of the house rather than tag-along visitor.

The Madam ends with a final flourish that leaves the quill poised above a well of ink. Her needle-sharp eyes study me, peering through the thick veil of her lashes. I fidget beneath her gaze until she smiles and turns towards the Captain with a raised eyebrow.

"And the boy?"

The Captain spins on his unsteady legs, stares at me through the haze of rum and ruin that accompanies him whenever we put ashore. He considers the question for a few moments, mocking finger to his pursed lips, the barest hint of a smile visible through the tangled mane of his beard.

"The boy? What do you say, Benjamin? Should we give

the boy his first tumble?"

Mr. Drummond scowls. He is a bookish man, despite his first-mate's bluster. Short and straight as a ramrod, still every bit a schoolmaster despite his years at sea. He gives the Captain a short nod, neat and efficient.

"Aye," he says. "Let the lad sample the wares, if he's fool enough to agree."

I am. Fool enough to agree, fool enough to seek this out, fool enough to abandon my London name and London comforts for the *Black Swallow* and a cabin boy's berth. Fool enough to risk my secrets, just to see the last of the Old Houses in action.

I'm fool enough, and I tell them so.

"Please, Captain."

There is a pause then, an empty lull that I've learned to recognize as the first sign of a coming storm. I can feel a thrill of fear run down my back, the hair on my neck standing to attention. The Captain's smile grows slowly; like the shoals of a hidden reef coming into view too late.

Mr. Drummond's face is a grim mask, concealing the clumsy knot of desire and loathing. Taciturn, is Mr. Drummond, and a pederast at the best of times. He has sought to take my innocence for the last year, despite the Captain's orders to the contrary.

The Madam waits patiently, the nib of her pen paused above the ledger. A bead of ink swells on the tip. I may not have the Madam's experience, but I have always been a quick study. I understand my place in this struggle, my role as a sharp knife used to tease the flesh of Ben Drummond's throat.

The Mate has thought our struggle beneath the Captain's notice. Ben Drummond has rarely needed to practice such subtlety; the buggery of cabin boys is common enough, even aboard respectable vessels. Had I set sail on another ship, under the command of any other captain, the question of my first tumble would have been decided long since and its tragic consequences already played out, for better or for worse.

I have been lucky with the *Black Swallow*, with her crew and her captain. Luckier than I deserve, fool that I am, so far from home in my thirteenth year. I force myself to affect excitement, an eagerness to see what lies beyond the velvet curtains. My stomach churns, a queasy roil worse than the sickness that plagued my first day on open water.

The Captain shifts his gaze between Mr. Drummond and me, leering as he fishes coins from their hiding place beneath his shirt.

"For the boy," he says, dropping a tarnished gold disk onto the Madam's creaking table. The Madam palms the coin, adds a flourishing X beside my name. Mr. Drummond's eyes draw deep into his skull.

"Yes," he says. "For the boy. May the whores treat him gentle on this special night."

There is laughter then, laughter from both men; Mr. Drummond's heaving cackle joining with the Captain's booming roar. A cold chill settles into my gut as the tension between them eases, the same chill I get when the *Swallow* is becalmed and laying fallow in the water.

There are times when it's better to weather the storm and see where it takes you, but I have heard the stories about the Old Houses and I know them better than any man aboard the *Swallow*. I have connived my way here, using Mr. Drummond's hunger as best I can, but I find myself suddenly afraid of what lies beyond.

The Captain claps my shoulder, pushing me towards the tattered velvet curtain. I draw a deep breath and step across the threshold, into the House of Pale Flowers, last of the great, old houses of Isla Tortuga, ready to find the twice-born whore who will transform Toby Truman forever.

~

The Madam leads us along the cobwebbed hall, along the floorboards that have been worn smooth with the rolling gait of a hundred thousand sailors, past the walls lined with the yellowed skulls of the dead. The Captain walks beside her, exaggerating his drunken stumble. Occasionally he reaches out, rubbing the cranium of an old friend, staining his fingers with bitter oil and dust. Mr. Drummond walks by my side, a quick march with a stiff back, eyes focused on the door at the far end, gazing down the impossible length of the hallway.

It's the noise that surprises me as we walk, the raucous roar of a drunken crowd dancing and singing to the quick beat of a rolling shanty. Something about the noise seems strangely inappropriate, given the stories that surround the Old Houses; every tale tells of the silent ladies, unable to utter a single word on pain of death, quiet as the graves they were rescued from, even in the throes of passion. It seems sacrilege to engage in such revels in their presence, an insult to their sacrifices, even if their customers have never put much faith in God or the church.

It was different once, if you believe the stories. They say the Old Houses were sacred places, the home of lost secrets and forbidden loves, everything a pirate needed to warm his waterlogged heart.

"You've picked a good night," the Madam says, pausing before the oak door that ends the hallway. "There is only a small crowd; if you'll amuse yourselves in the parlor for a time, our girls will be with you shortly."

Then she pushes the door open and the roar of the

parlor is doubled; it hits us like a cannon's retort, impossibly loud and stung with a sudden flash of heat. The parlor stinks of pipe smoke and hot blood, the broken voices of sea-faring men singing along with an off-key piano.

I once heard a crewman call this place the last great house of ill-repute, his voice full of quiet reverence, but I see little to revere in the human flotsam that litters this room. They fill the overstuffed divans and driftwood tables, with grey-fleshed girls limping on twisted legs or serving drinks with an arm that has been broken and poorly set before healing.

A dead girl emerges from the throng, ready to lead us to the table. Her left eye is missing; the flesh around the empty cavity an angry and puckered scar. She holds forward three fingers, then waves her hand to indicate we should follow. As she turns, I can see the clumsy stitching that has repaired a wound to the back of her skull. It looks deep; like the aftermath of an axe-blow or the crushing weight of an iron belaying pin. The stitches hold the black flesh closed, barely concealing the rot at the seam.

Mr. Drummond strides past me, following her as she cuts through the crowd of flesh. I hesitate for a moment, hands on my ears, trying not to breath in the scent of unwashed sailors and death. The weight of the Captain's arm settles across my shoulders, his thin lips drawing close to my ears.

"Relax," he says. "They use the broken girls as waitresses; the pretty ones are kept for the back rooms."

I nod. The Captain offers me a wide grin, his first genuine smile of the evening.

"Come," he says, breath hot against the side of my face. "First we'll drink, then we'll make merry. You'll forget that they're dead soon enough."

He guides me into the throng with a steady hand. We move carefully through the press of bodies, pausing so the captain can greet old friends he finds among the crowd. Mr. Drummond has ordered by the time we reach the table, the waitress depositing three copper mugs filled with the Captain's favored concoction of rum and gunpowder.

"To your health," the Captain says. He throws his head back and takes a long draught.

Mr. Drummond doesn't drink at first, simply sits with his back to the wall, eyes darting as he sweeps the crowd for familiar faces. He is a cautious man, hiding his nerves behind a scowl, always searching for those that would do him harm.

The Captain deposits me in a seat by the wall, the seat closest to Ben Drummond and his eyes of cold flint. Deposited me here with a quick wink and a leer of pure joy, a leer that assures me I have little choice in my position. His game continues, until he says otherwise. It's closer to Mr. Drummond than I've been in a year, closer than I'd want to be under normal circumstances.

I stoop in my seat, a clammy sense of fear in the pit of my stomach.

Mr. Drummond leans his skinny weight onto the scarred driftwood of the tabletop. He steeples his fingers, holding them before his mouth, a lingering gesture from his days as a man of learning.

"Relax," he says, soft enough that the Captain can barely hear. "You've got nothing to fear from me, not here."

I nod, once, but it does little to quell the nerves. There have been incidences aplenty aboard the *Swallow*, despite the Captain's close watch, too many close calls for me to take Mr. Drummond at his word. He makes a rough gurgle in the depths of his throat, a sound that's almost a sigh, and he turns his cold eyes towards me.

"Relax, Toby Truman," he says. "There are darker pleasures in this world than you can offer, and plenty here to satiate even my appetites. The Old Houses are dangerous enough without worrying about me. Save your trembling for something that deserves it."

There are stories aplenty about Ben Drummond, tales as dark and unfriendly as any you've heard over a midsummer campfire. They say he tutored a governor's child once, before his appetites forced him to take to the sea. They say he's been banished from ship after ship, cast off for deeds that even a buccaneer crew could not sanction. They say a great deal, these stories I've heard, and they imply much that is worse.

But the stories of the Old Houses are darker still, and the stories about the Pale Flower are often darkest of them all, so I choose to believe him, just this once. I let myself relax, let myself lean back into the rickety comfort of my chair and sip my drink while the Captain's order fills the table with rum and brandy and pipes filled with opium and fine tobacco.

The Captain breathes a white plume into the air, exhaling smoke like a contented dragon as we watch the crowd thin and disappear into the back rooms of the bordello. He has his boot propped on the driftwood table, a wooden cup dangling lazily from his fingers.

I take my time and study the crowd, watching even the bravest sailor flinch when he's forced to address one of the silent waitresses. They are mangled creatures, the victims of violent deaths, brought back with hurried stitching and missing parts. Mournful, misshapen creatures; women who have been destroyed by their deal with the black spirits that sponsor the Old Houses.

There are few men who are truly comfortable here, though the Old Houses have been pirate dens since the first buccaneer set foot upon the shore. They flinch and they look away, unwilling to deal with the walking dead regardless of their anxious glances towards the curtains and the whore's boudoirs. They are men who are plagued by fear, drinking and dancing only to escape the inevitable. It isn't long before I wonder why they've come.

Only the Captain seems truly at home. He revels in the promise of debauchery, in the willing violation of the natural order that the Pale Flower represents.

Mr. Drummond does not revel, though he hides it well. His face is old leather, stretched across the skull, perfect for hiding the minutia of expression. He drinks cautiously, refusing the Captain's offer to share a pipe, stays alert to the impending possibilities of the evening. His drinks are pushed to my corner of the table, pushed across with quiet gestures he believes the Captain does not notice.

"Drink," Mr. Drummond tells me. "It will help with your nerves."

I drink a little, choking on the angry tang of rum. I keep my eyes on the serving girls, on their horrific wounds and scars, on the heavy curtains that occasionally part and allow one of the throng access to the back rooms and the ladies who dwell there. On the grimace of fear and confusion that flashes across each patron's face, as though unsure exactly why they're taking the next step.

"Captain," I say. "They look afraid."

The Captain is drunk now, truly drunk rather than some feigned act. He roars with laughter.

"Of course they're afraid," the Captain says, his roar cutting through the crowd like a shark's fin. "They don't know the secret. There is an art to loving an Old House harlot. Don't you agree, Mr. Drummond?"

Mr. Drummond gives a short, crowing laugh.

"He doesn't believe me," the Captain says.

"It would appear not, Captain."

The Captain's lip curls into a sly smile, his eyes shining through the smoke haze.

"That's Ben's choice," he says. "His to make, despite the danger."

"Danger, Captain?" Mr. Drummond says.

"Danger," the Captain says. "Though not the type you'd think. True, there is always danger when sleeping with a woman, no matter who she may be. But the ladies of the Old Houses are different, they get beneath your skin. The memory of them gnaws at you during the lonely nights at sea, nibbling away your soul until there's nothing left. Therein lies the art; learning to love them while the opportunity presents itself, then letting the memory go before it destroys you."

Mr. Drummond scowls, thick brows meeting above his hooked nose.

"Love, Captain?" he says. "Love is the stuff of poetry and children's tales, not the base currency of the Old Houses. Where does one find love here, among the dead?"

The Captain smiles, touches a finger to the side of his nose.

"Love is inescapable, Mr. Drummond, even in the Old Houses. For we are creatures married to the sea, unfit for loving ordinary women. The ladies are dead and reborn, unfit for loving an ordinary man. We are all outcasts in the eyes of god, so we love each other as best we can. It may not be the love of your poems and fairy tales, I'll grant you that, but what they offer us is true enough for my purposes."

"You're a romantic."

"Who isn't, these days? We all bear the mark of

romance, though we hide it like the first signs of plague." The Captain peers at us from beneath the brim of his hat. "Take note, young Toby, Mr. Drummond may doubt me, but he hasn't yet said that I'm wrong."

Mr. Drummond snorts, taking a long draught from his cup. He places it, empty, on the table.

"Misguided," he says. "But not wrong. It was different, once, before the Frenchman and his army of street-whores."

He stands and inclines his head, calling our attention to the curtain leading into the rear rooms. The Madam is waiting there. I can make out a cluster of girls behind her, pale and regal, resplendent in shimmering gowns and their necklaces of silver and gold. Overdressed for harlots, but the Old Houses have always known that women and wealth go hand in hand when it comes to raising a pirate's ardor.

"It's time," Mr. Drummond says. For the first time I can hear a slight current of fear below the croak of his voice. His left hand, his whipping hand, flexes and curls in anticipation of what is to come. "My advice, boy, should you want to take it; get what you need, leave everything else behind. Remember that you sleep with the dead tonight, and there's precious little you can do to change that. Any feeling you see in them is just a hopeful figment, wished into being by your own desires, as ethereal and intangible as mist on the sea."

It is the Captain who selects my partner, a dark-haired girl named Beatrice with skin as pale and clear as the china dolls I played with as a child. She leads me into a boudoir that smells of clove incense and stale sweat; a heavy fugue that hangs in the smoky air, so thick I can barely see the rafters above us.

Beatrice holds my hand between her cold fingers, leads me into the heart of the smoke where a lounge and bed lays waiting. Her cold hands guide me, seating me on the plump lounge whose leather is ripped and rent.

"Sit," she says, and I am so shocked that I do so with mouth agape, like a wounded fish sucking for air upon the deck.

"Would you care for a drink? Something to smoke? We have some fine opium, if you'd prefer it?"

Her voice is unnaturally dark and rich, a sombre funeral dirge chafing to break into a lively waltz once the audience's back is turned. I shake my head, mute, and she arranges herself with languorous grace upon the threadbare cushions of the bed.

"You can talk," I tell her, and I'm sure there's a quaver in my voice as I do so. She nods, smiling at me, her lips drawing into a winsome curve that belies her idle authority in this exchange. I feel a sharp heat rising into my cheeks.

"The ladies of the Old Houses do not talk," I tell her. "They are silent as the graves they were rescued from, and nearly as trustworthy when it comes to keeping a man's secrets."

She shrugs, a practiced gesture that sees her bosom heave with fluid grace.

"We do not speak to men," she says. "A necessity of the contract, but one that's good for business."

"Then why speak to me?"

She shrugs again. I wince, suddenly aware of how complacent I've been so long at sea, so long undiscovered and surrounded by men. It is easy to hide among sailors, men unfamiliar with women beyond a few trysts at shore, willing to see a boy simply because they cannot imagine anything but in my place.

The skin at the base of my neck itches, my face is scarlet. I am not yet ready to return home, to abandon the sea and take up the safe life my mother planned for me. The dead girl revels in my discomfort.

"There must be some mistake," I tell her, doing my best to keep the nerves from my voice.

"There must," Beatrice agrees. "Though it is strange, is it not? That a lady of the old houses can talk to a man? Break the compact without the specter of death coming to claim her?"

"Strange," I agree. Beatrice shrugs a third time, letting the slit of her robe fall open a little wider. The flesh of her chest is smooth and pale as cream, marred only by the livid scar of a bullet hole next to her left breast. I find myself tempted to reach out, to stroke the vivid knot of poorly healed skin.

"Perhaps," Beatrice says. "Stranger things have happened, in a house such as this."

She turns, drawing her robe closed, the legacy of her first death disappearing beneath layers of crimson silk.

I draw my feet up, hugging my knees close to my chest, feeling childish for the first time in months.

"So," I say, quietly.

"So," Beatrice agrees. Her voice is like liquor now, lush and harsh and heavy with promise.

"What happens next?"

"Traditionally, there is an exchange," Beatrice says. "We do what is necessary to sate your desires, or what we can do, to that end, in the time we have. Some men remain a work in progress."

"And then?"

"And then we are done," she says. "Then you go on

your way, sailing off on your ship, and the memory of our time together gnaws at you, just as your captain promised. It gnaws at your soul and nibbles at your dreams and swallows you whole in order to pay my tithe."

"Just like that?"

"Just like that," she says, gravely, her voice devoid of mockery. "It is something of a sacred duty."

"And what happens if you fail?" I ask her. "What happens if I come here desiring nothing?"

Beatrice smiles, leaning forward as though preparing to whisper a final secret. I lean in, close enough to taste the sea-salt and pickling wine that lingers beneath the heavy scent of her perfume.

"Everyone desires something," she says. "They don't come here if they don't."

One pale hand curls around my hair, drawing me closer. She kisses me and her lips taste like gravestones, like sodden dirt mixed with warm copper, like the hunger of a starving man.

It is a good kiss, powerful, a lure to reel me into the unfamiliar territory of her bed. I know better than to follow, but it takes more strength that I have to resist.

I succumb, briefly. We do not make love, though I allow Beatrice to unravel the tattered strips of my disguise. We do not make love, but her cold hands caress my face, my ribs, the hollows of my knee. We do not make love, but her kiss is cold against my lips and filled with promises.

For a moment I allow myself to feel hopeless within her grasp, writhing and twisting like a fish on the line that knows it will be drawn up onto the deck. Then it is over, halted, nothing more than a momentary weakness. Beatrice lays my head on the pillow, gently wraps me in the cold shadow of her embrace.

We lie together, quietly, a narrow shiver running the

length of my spine. She has discarded her robe, allowing me to see the puckered scar once more, a ghost pale reminder of a pistol shot to the heart. This time I do reach out, tracing the knotted flesh with my finger. It's strangely warm, as though touched by some lingering spark of fire from the lead slug that ended her life.

"Did you know them?" I ask; it's an incautious question, one that takes her off-guard. Beatrice looks down, presses her finger against the old wound, rubbing it lightly with her cold hands.

"I knew them," she says, finally, her voice little more than a whisper. "Not well, perhaps, but well enough."

"Do you remember?" I ask. "I mean, you hear stories, girls sold to the Old Houses before their times; still living, even if they're told otherwise; their flesh left cold and clammy by magic, to give the illusion of the grave."

Beatrice smiles gently. I notice, for the first time, the reddish tinge of old blood on her teeth.

"I remember enough," she says. "It isn't something you'd recall clearly, given the choice, but I remember enough to be sure. To know that they brought me back, called me home to uphold my side of our bargain, bound me with silence and duty in exchange for my life."

A cold thumb presses itself against my forehead, resting in the space between my eyes.

"Where do you hear such stories, little pirate?"

It's my turn to shrug.

"And why are you interested? What do you care for the poor, dead girls of Isla Tortuga?"

Beatrice studies me. There are stories about eyes and windows, so I know enough to close my own, to lock away the memories of my mother and her pale flesh, of the nightmares she offered me as bedtime stories until I was old enough to run away. Some days I can still hear her echo, all the old warnings she offered me, explaining that the world was a cold place for women and a colder place for a courtesan's child.

With closed eyes I permit myself to remember my mother; her violet eyes, the soothing chill of her hands, the ghostly heartbeat that made a lie of her graveyard pallor.

She hated my love of the sea, my infatuation with pirates and sailors, my soul that would not be tamed by books and tutors and the fruits of her wealth.

But it was a cold hatred, the final ember of an extinguished fire, trapped beneath the eternal frost that chilled both her body and soul. I sometimes wonder if she wept when she discovered her child was a runaway. It seems unlikely.

Beatrice is staring when I open my eyes, still waiting for an answer. I look at her, catching a glimpse of ghostly memories hemmed in behind her grey pupils. I see pain and sorrow and not enough joy, the same echoes that lived in my mother's head, buried deep beneath the sultry languor of her eternal stare. Beatrice gives me a slow smile, disarming in its honesty. We have both given something away here, letting our secrets live a little closer to the surface that we'd like.

When she speaks, her voice is little more than a whisper: "How long have you been at sea, Tobias Truman?"

And though it has only been a year and three months, it still feels like forever, the weight of the days bunching like a clenched fist deep in my chest. Beatrice touches a tear as it rolls down my face, holds it before me on the tip of her lily-white finger.

"This is not an answer, little pirate?"

"Maybe not," I tell her. "But everyone has the secrets, and the wise sell them as dearly as they can."

I have been gathering tears for a year now, hoarding them up like my own private ocean. Beatrice takes me in her arms, cooing quietly as I scatter her bed with my gathered sorrow, a hundred tiny shards of salt-water that I dare not carry back to the sea when I leave.

~

Beatrice shows me to the hall when our time is done, closing her door behind me with a gentle smile and a farewell kiss. The Madam waits nearby, ready to lead me away. It's a long hall, lined with doors, each leading to another boudoir, another pirate, another dead girl playing at life. I listen carefully as the Madam leads me past them, straining my ears to pick up every heaving breath and grunting drive as client after client expends his seed. There are no women among the voices, no matter how I strain, just masculine moans and manly groans as the moment of climax is reached.

For a moment, barely longer than the space of three breaths, I could swear I hear Mr. Drummond's hollow cackle. The sound is followed by the familiar snap of the lash, the wet sound of flesh flaying off bone. My steps falter, causing the Madam to pause. She looks down at me, her eyebrow raised.

"Any desire," she says. "It's the role of the Old Houses. We try to fulfill any desire, and we take what we need in return. He cannot hurt them."

"He wants to," I tell her. "He wants to hear them scream."

The Madam offers me an elegant shrug.

"The dead do not scream," she says. "They do not speak, they do not sigh, they are silent as the grave. This is immutable, even in the face of desire."

"So I've been told," I tell her. "But they could speak, if they wanted to. They could give him what they wanted."

The Madam regards me carefully, silent as the night. We stand there, amid the whisper of a dozen clients behind closed doors, the muted buzz of the lounge in the distance.

Eventually the Madam nods.

"They could," she says, "but they won't. It would be the end, the talking; no man would come here, once the secrets are revealed."

She stares at me, her eyes ancient behind the thick layers of make-up.

"Do you understand, little pirate? Do you know what I'm saying?"

There is a flicker of breeze in the hallway, setting the candle's dancing. I think of my mother, powdered and cold, living out her life under my father's thumb. She wore the mask of a lady as it suited her, but there were precious few disguises that concealed her true nature.

I look the Madam in the eyes and nod.

"Reputations must be maintained," I tell her.

The Madam smiles.

"Yes," she says. "I suppose they must."

Then she takes my arm and she walks, returning me to the velvet curtain and the lounge beyond.

The revel has been tempered by the passing of time, whittling away both noise and numbers until the room is near empty and the voices muted.

The Captain is waiting for me, feet on the table, broad smile clamped around an ancient pipe. I sit down at the table, taking a long swallow of the mug he pushes into my hands. It's warm and harsh, like drinking fish scales.

"So that's that," he says. "Was it everything you expected, after the stories you've heard?"

I shrug, unsettled, wondering if I've left some gap in

my disguise.

"Nothing is ever what you expect of it," I tell him. "Why should this place be any different?"

The Captain nods, the feather on his hat weaving a solemn dance; he pulls his feet off the table with a single fluid gesture, climbing to his feet.

"Mr. Drummond will not likely emerge before dawn," the Captain says. "It's probably best that we don't wait. We should return to the ship, let you get a good nights sleep while you can. We break port in two days, and he's always worse after a night in Tortuga."

I nod, getting ready to follow him. The Captain lays an arm over my shoulder as I stand.

"Did you find what you were looking for, Tobias Truman?"

He gives me a wolfish smile, but his eyes are serious beneath the brim of his hat. I consider the question for a long moment, studying it as though he'd asked my opinion of a precious jewel. "Perhaps," I tell him. "But at least we can be sure that I got what I wanted."

He nods and I savor his interest, his desire to treat me as part of his crew; I'm acutely aware, even now, that it cannot last forever. I will get older, and with age comes secrets I can no longer hide.

I do not have the stomach for a lady-pirates life, fighting to hold my place among the crew.

"What about you, Captain, did you get what you wanted?"

The Captain smiles at me.

"Nothing more, nothing less," he says. "Just as they promise."

And he leads me out of the room, into the streets of Isla Tortuga, back to the ship that I can call home a little longer.

ON THE DESTRUCTION OF COPENHAGEN BY THE WAR-MACHINES OF THE MERFOLK

1.

When it starts we're in a hotel room, the two of us curled up on a double bed. It's a two-star kind of place: cracks in the walls, curtains covered in faded daisies, the clinging smell of camphor attaching itself after the first few of minutes of your stay. The television stutters as we flick through the channels, colors bleeding together and rendering the devastation a fuzzy blue or green. Still, we see it happen: the great machines of the merfolk coming up over the shore, rampaging through the city with devastating effect. We watch a robotic mermaid hammer her fist into an apartment block, the dust cloud from the explosion engulfing the nearby camera. It's quick, sudden, a surprise that's ruined by the later repetition of the footage. We breathe in and all we can smell are mothballs. It's almost a disappointment.

We're not in Copenhagen, but it's possible my sister is. She was there when last I talked to her, and I don't know when she was leaving. My knowledge of her trip consists entirely of reports on the quality of her breakfast. I don't know when she was planning on leaving the city, but I know Copenhagen makes excellent waffles and cream. This knowledge, once gathered, proves to be useless. I explain all this to the girl beside me, and she looks up, wide-eyed. She asks if this means we'll be going home early, just in case. I think about it, and then: *No*, I tell her. *No, of course not. There's nothing I can do at home that I can't do here.*

This is selfish, I know, but I console myself with the knowledge that my sister doesn't stay places for longer than a few days. She was going to Iceland next, and there's a good chance she's moved on. I say as much, when pressed. *Iceland*, I say. *Odds are, she's in Iceland. Nothing to worry about unless we hear otherwise.*

The girl beside me asks *why Iceland?* I tell her I have no idea. My sister's travels are guided by a logic she doesn't share with others.

2.

I won't leave you in suspense. That would be unfair. My sister didn't make it to Iceland. Her flight was cancelled on account of the attack. No one tells us this. My sister doesn't call. In the absence of news, my mother panics. She leaves worried messages on my cell phone. I do not panic. I place my trust in my sister's ability to take care of herself, even in the face of vast robotic war-machines and cancelled flights.

My sister carries trouble with her like luggage, always ready to be unpacked. It's a habit that's given her plenty of experience surviving the unexpected.

3.

My date is only twenty-two. I'm almost thirty-five. We don't tell people that we're going out. Her name is Hayley, though this is probably a lie. She thinks my name is Dean, though she is unsure of whether this is a Christian name, a surname, or a nom-de-plume.

The best thing about Hayley: she smells like cotton candy. Lying in bed with her, smelling her hair, is frequently better than our stilted attempts to have sex.

Hayley has a cobra tattooed on her left arm in green ink. She has a blue mermaid tattoo on her right thigh. She sent me photographs of both when we were flirting online, but the cobra seems more threatening when seen in real life. Hayley met me at the hotel wearing cut-off jeans and a tank top, all her ink on display for the whole world to see. I paid the hotel room while she watched me through the glass door. We checked in as Mister and Miss Dean.

In theory, we are both engineers. This is the occupation both of us offered, when the question was raised online. We bonded over this, our mutual interest in machines. It greased the early days of our relationship admirably.

We are liars, and we assume as much. This is a basic precaution in the age of the Internet. Yet both of us enjoy the game more than we let on.

4.

My parents text me, pinging my cell every couple of minutes. Text messages are a bad way to communicate in an emergency. They would seem comical if I wasn't watching the news, even though my parents aren't known for their sense of whimsy. I read their messages to Hayley during the lull in the news reports: *Have you heard from your sister? There's a giant robot mermaid crawling through Copenhagen. It's fighting its way to the Christiansborg Palace! Do you remember the name of your sister's hotel? Do you remember the name of your sister's airline? Have you heard from her since this started? My god, did you see the damage that tail caused? Have you heard from your sister? Has she tried to give you a call? Why aren't you answering your phone?*

5.

We don't hear from my sister for three days. Then we do. She leaves a message on my phone: *Not dead, not in Iceland, everything okay. Give you call when I get home.* I forward this message to my mother and scan the limited breakfast options on the hotel's room-service menu. Hayley and I order raisin toast that comes with not enough butter. Hayley tells me this is her favorite breakfast ever, the only thing she can eat at the start of the day.

6.

It emerges that no-one knows why the attack took place. The merfolk's statement on the matter is a collection of high-pitched whale songs that remain difficult to decipher, so people develop their own theories to make sense of the destruction. My favorite suggests that perhaps, in retrospect, the statue of the Little Mermaid in Copenhagen harbor may have been something of a mistake; that the merfolk may have taken it for some kind of taunt.

My sister visited that statue three times in the past. Each time, she says, regardless of the season or clothing she's wearing, it's the coldest place she's ever been. My sister has been to many cold places. She has seen both the

Arctic and Antarctic circles. She is not sorry to hear that the statue was torn down in the wake of the attack.

7.

It should be noted that visiting Iceland is still on my sister's to-do list, thanks to this horrible tragedy.

8.

There are some people, my friends among them, who will believe the destruction of Copenhagen is an urban myth. Others will believe it's a cover up for something both more mundane and infinitely more sinister. They will blame the Americans. America is easy to blame in moments like this.

My sister suffered three injuries during the attack, though all of them were minor. The worst was a sprained right ankle, which ballooned up and forced her to limp along on crutches for a week before it healed. She sent me photographs of her injuries, her ankle dark and swollen like she's hiding a storm cloud beneath her skin.

The photographs of my sister's ankle will do little to convince those who doubt the attack ever truly happened. They will tell me such injuries could have happened to anyone, at any time, and I cannot prove them wrong.

9.

There were five robots in Copenhagen. I told Hayley they were simultaneously works of innovative engineering and one of the poorest designs I had ever seen. She snuggled close and asked me to explain. I closed my eyes and breathed in the smell of her hair.

The genius of the robots was in their scale: two

hundred feet tall and strong enough to smash a building into rubble. The merfolk did this using parts scavenged from sunken ships, each robot a patchwork construct made from metal and waterlogged wood. That the robots worked at all is a marvel, requiring foresight and ingenuity that few human engineers could match.

The flaws of the robots lay in their scales: the use of the merfolk as the base form, rather than a creature adapted for movement on land. Each war machine was covered in a scaled shell of metal that leaked water every time the robot moved, forcing them to return to the ocean at periodic intervals where they would sink beneath the surface as a flurry of air-bubbles boiled the water. This flaw ensured the rampage was limited to a small section of the Copenhagen shoreline.

Hayley was impressed by my observations, commenting on my insight. I told her I never wanted to be smart; I wanted to be free to travel the world on a whim, just like my sister.

10.

The games we play to pass the time: Hayley is an Italian maid and I'm the horny tourist she walks in on. She's a stunning French philosophy student and I'm the horny waiter at her favorite café. She's a terrified Danish film star and I'm the rampaging robot that picks her up and fights off the air force while clinging to the side of Copenhagen's tallest tower.

Then news reports tell us that the rampage is over, that the robots ranged too far from the shore, leaving the pilots gasping for air inside the dormant constructs.

11.

They announce the final death toll. It's lower than either of us expected. We pack up and go home the next day. The war with the merfolk is over.

12.

The next time I see Hayley she will be older, wiser, less prone to dating men that she meets on the internet. Her hair will smell like something other than cotton candy. We will spot one another at opposite ends of the cereal aisle at the supermarket. I will be reaching for Coco Puffs; she will be reaching for name-brand muesli. I will be fatter and growing a beard, and I will stop myself from calling out her name when I see her standing next to a friend who may-or-may-not know of Hayley's double life as Hayley-the-Engineer. I will feel a sudden surge of jealousy: Hayley's friend will know if her name isn't really Hayley, but I will never know. My arm will falter. I will smile instead. Hayley will smile back. She will excuse herself and hurry down the aisle so she can kiss me on the cheek. She will ask after my sister. I will tell her my sister is fine, thought she's currently stuck in Korea, paying off an impressive bar tab generated during a wild night at an underground casino. We will laugh at that. We will not mention our time together. Hayley will excuse herself. She will go back and start talking to her friend, making some comment that explains who I am without mentioning the fact that we once dated.

The merfolk will have gone underground, censured by the global community for their actions in Denmark. The oceans will be deemed unsafe. We will worry about ships lost at sea; each new incident will become global news. We will lose faith in our navy. Hayley will rejoin her friend. She will choose a more expensive brand of muesli and place it in her shopping cart. I will watch the two of them go, walking away from me, disappearing around the corner of the aisle. I will admire the curve of Hayley's back. I will wonder if Hayley was ever her real name. I will close my eyes and wish. I will wish that we could sleep together, just one more time. I will wish we were back in the hotel room, that the merfolk invasion could start again. Hayley will be gone. I will miss her. I will wish she still smelt like cotton candy, and I will breathe in the sugar-sweet smell of the Coco-Puffs and pretend that I'm smelling her for a little while longer.

Later I will remember that my sister still hasn't made it to Iceland. It's the one place I can still go that she has never been.

THE SEVENTEEN EXECUTIONS OF SIGNORE DON VASHTA

1.

Of the sixteen recorded executions featuring Signore Don Vashta as the subject, I have been present for three, and I have read detailed and verified accounts of another two.

In addition, I am known as a man who has an interest in such things, and thus I am a man to whom all rumors eventually find their way. Among our fraternity, if we can truly be called such, this makes me something of an expert, and I do not take this duty lightly.

As many of you know, I inherited this particular interest from one Roland K., who lived in the Americas and served as my mentor. It is with respect to the fidelity and accuracy of Roland's service that I leave this note to explain my most recent actions.

2.

Roland K. once sent a letter from his station in the Americas. In it, he detailed the events that led to his resignation, and the dismissal from our ledgers that followed not long after.

"It is a terrible thing to hang a man," his letter said, *"and I find I have no longer have the stomach for it, particularly in the manner that is utilized in these parts. There is no art to death here, no science as precise as the hangman's drop. There are no scaffolds to serve as the staging for the death, nor even the grotesque parody offered by a rope looped over a convenient branch. Instead they affix the noose to the top of a great pole and raise the subject to it, hoisting him into position using a sling affixed beneath the arms.*

"The subjects own weight is enough to begin the process, although it is slower than we have come to prefer. When the locals wish to hasten the subject's death, a second noose is placed over the feet and several strong men pull down, speeding the asphyxiation that inevitably results in death. This is, despite the barbarism involved, the more humane method of execution given the limitations of their method.

"They did no such thing when Signore Vashta came to the noose.

"It's not the act that disables me so, but the anticipation of it. There is so much waiting, Beal, so much pageantry. Signore Vashta's crimes were minor, and he stood, resolute, while the theatre of death played out. It's a terrible thing we do, Beal, a terrible, terrible thing. Those minutes he stood on the platform, adorned with noose and a black sack to obscure his features. Minutes spent listening, waiting, while the sling was placed around him.

"It is the sound of it that haunts me, my friend. The gurgle and croak of a man left to die. It is a terrible thing to be haunted, in our work.

"For days after the execution, I believed I saw the dead man dallying about town, seated in cafes or breaking his fast at the local hotel. I told myself that it cannot be, that the dead, of necessity, stay dead, and yet Signore Don Vashta's shade persists, an ever-present reminder of the things I have witnessed.

"I fear I can no longer perform my duties. My reason becomes

suspect, and our work must remain above reproach if we are to be trusted."

It is a matter of public record that Roland K. tendered his resignation two weeks after the mailing of this letter, and there are many who impugn his reputation when they speculate on his reasons for doing so.

I share these details with you today because his letter brings to light many things that I, too, have noticed in my years following Signore Vashta and his many executions.

It is true, as Roland K. notes, that it is not natural to kill a man, even one who cannot die such as Signore Don Vashta. It is true, as he notes, that a measure of pageantry is necessary. The pageantry creates the distance one needs to go through with the act, serves as the barrier between the executioner and despair.

We are protected by reason and the understanding of our role, both of which are threatened when Don Vashta returns from the grave.

3.

My own meeting with Signore Vashta took place here in the antipodes, when he was first incarcerated in the dismal Melbourne Jail, awaiting his inevitable demise at the hands of Her Majesty's firing squad.

It was, at the time, two days before his scheduled execution.

It should be noted that the firing squad was not the preferred method of execution in Melbourne at the time - any study of our records will show the locals shared a predilection for the noose - but even then Don Vashta's abilities were known to the local correctional.

And so an expert was called for, and so it became my

duty to advise them on the correct procedures for elimination.

Don Vashta knew my role immediately, from the moment I entered his cell, and he rose from the Spartan cot to greet me like an old friend, kissing me upon each cheek before clasping me to his chest. "Sir," he said, whispering so that I alone could hear him, "whatever you do tomorrow, do your duty. I must demand that you kill me, for I fear I am a villain and cannot be trusted to continue walking this earth."

I told him, as we all do, that it is not our place to punish the accused. We act from a place of reason, doing as duty demands. We leave it to others to apportion blame and decide the guilty's punishment.

Don Vashta seemed to grasp this, and released me from his grip. "Do not fear, sir," he said. "I welcome any man who can finally end my time here on earth. When your men shoot--" he paused to thump his chest with a fist "--aim here, aim true, I beg you."

It was, I learned, to be his fourth execution, although only the second to use the firing squad as their means of disposal. He'd last faced such a punishment in the early days of the First World War, and it had proved no more effective than the morning he was hung.

I asked him, years later, why he expected my squad to succeed where others had already failed.

"Ah, Beal," he said, and lifted an ice-cooled drink to his lips. "I no longer desired to live, my friend, by the time the two of us met. I believed that would make the difference, and in that I was twice a fool."

4.

I will note, here, that Signore Vashta is prettier than one might expect after hearing of his legend. His eyelashes are long and delicate as a woman's, and his lips are thin and exquisite in their cruelty. We shall not speak of his blade-like cheeks, nor the endless sorrow in his eyes. Only the loss of his left ear mars the symmetry of his features, and even that is normally covered by the habit of growing his hair long.

On the night before his seventh execution, he asked me for a woman. We were in the Americas, and my presence in his cell was purely a courtesy. I had no power here, far from home, beyond my familiarity with the subject and my reputation as an expert in his condition. They wanted me present to advise them and ensure the execution took. My response was that there could be no such guarantee, but they flew me over anyway and put me up in a cheap motel a few minutes away from the prison.

"If it's to be my last night," Don Vashta said, "I would rather like a woman to see me off to whatever comes next. I don't suppose you could organize that, Beal?"

"That is not in my power," I told him, and he sighed and nodded.

"I would go myself," he said, "but, well, you know." He waved his hands at the bars, at the concrete walls and the prison guards, the cameras that watched his ever movement.

"I never had problems getting women, Beal," he said. "Perhaps that is part of my curse, eh?

"You are a handsome man, Signore."

"I am," he agreed, "but I'll not be so pretty tomorrow." He sniffed and lay his head against the thin pillows of his cot. "Pity."

I could not tell you what moved me, this time and this time alone, but I made him an offer: "I could ask them to try poison instead. It will be considerably less messy."

Signore Vashta shook his head. "For a man of my proclivities," he said, "not being pretty is one of the few punishments the law can afford. There will be other women eventually, Beal, unless we finally get this right."

He smiled at me, and winked, then rolled over to go to sleep. I waited there through the evening, in case he had more to say.

The next morning they took him to the chamber. I sat in a small, concrete room with a governor and a lawyer and a weeping woman I could not recognize. At 10:15 the lights in the room flickered, and for the space of several minutes afterwards we let ourselves believe that this time, yes, this time, Don Vashta was truly dead.

5.

Signore Vashta lost his right ear during his third execution. It was torn off by a noose that was incorrectly applied, and this alone, of all his maladies, remains uncured and unhealed in the aftermath. I have long believed that solving the riddle of this scar, understanding why it alone remains with him, lies at the heart of resolving the problem Don Vashta represents.

Alas, I no longer have theories on how this scarring achieved. It is, like many things, a mystery beyond my understanding.

6.

By the eve of his thirteenth execution, it had become known amongst our fraternity that I was a man with an interest. There would be letters, sometimes as many as three in a week, from those who claimed to be present at Signore Don Vashta's final death. Many of these proved to be false, a charlatan's attempting to impress me with their made-up tales, or misguided efforts by junior members with too much faith in their skills.

One letter, in all those years, bore the ring of truth.

"My dear Beal," it began, *"I am writing to inform you of the most extraordinary incidents that accompanied the execution of a rogue known as Don Vashta, which I have been led to believe, by the friend of a friend, may be of some considerable interest to you.*

"I understand that you are familiar with the man I speak of - a rake and villain of considerable charm - and have previously served as an advisor for those in my position. He has been accused of great crimes in my country, and such crimes are punishable by beheading when the perpetrator is caught. Though it took us many moths, we acquired Signore Vashta while he broke his fast in a small cantina on the coast.

"It is my understanding that he came quite peacefully, despite having eaten only one of the three hard-boiled eggs he had ordered.

"We knew of him by reputation, although reputations are lacking in details, as I'm sure you are aware. It wasn't until I saw the scars on Signore Vashta's body, fading despite the application of a lash just three days before, that I truly believed such a man could exist. I did not believe in immortality, and still I do not, but perhaps some mark of the devil accompanies the criminal Vashta and saves him when others will perish.

"It was a humid morning when it came time to do my duty. Ordinarily we would have favored the gallows, but we knew there was no joy in attempting such a death. The task of finding a death that would finally bring Signore Vashta peace fell to me.

"I feel a great shame in my final decision, although I spoke with Don Vashta before implementing it. We fed him great quantities of acid, of the hydrochloric kind, a method I borrowed from a

particularly lurid novella I read in my childhood years. It was horrible to do, worse to experience, but in the final moments I believed I'd succeeded where other's failed. Don Vashta had been executed, although it was a cruel and debased death.

"I could not have done this to him, had he not asked me to do so. He wanted to die, badly, and no longer believed you would help him do so.

"We interred him in a traitor's grave. For days we believed he remained there, dead as any other victim of the executioner's art.

"Before the week was out we heard rumors of his presence in the countryside, feasting at the same cantina where we'd acquired him a week earlier. Upon hearing this, I went to see him. He spoke with a cold rasp, so it seems my cruelty had left some faint mark upon him and I had not the heart to report his presence to my superiors.

"I may be a patriot, Mister Beal, but I am not cruel. No matter what Don Vashta has done, I do not wish him to experience such pain again.

"I told him I would not arrest him again, although I begged him to leave the country. Eventually he agreed, and suggested I contact you to explain my actions.

"I do so now, although it shames me to make this admission. You have my respect, sir, for sticking with Don Vashta's case for so long as you have, particularly in light of the inevitable hopelessness of your cause.

"Yours, F."

I did not respond to Monsignor F.'s letter. There was little I could offer him that would make sense of what he'd seen.

7.

I have no record of Don Vashta's fourteenth execution, but I still hope to hear of the method used. It is one of three gaps in my otherwise comprehensive file.

8.

His fifteenth execution saw him drawn and quartered by a quartet of wild brumbies. An impromptu response to an insult he offered a local while the two us travelled through South America. I can still remember the look of glee on his face as they took him out and secured the chains on his wrists and ankles.

"Don't you understand, Beal? After all this time? At last, we have some novelty."

He grinned as they fired their rifles and the horses startled, bolting in all four directions. Signore Vashta was not a big man. It didn't take long for the horses to do their job.

It was here, we discovered, that dismemberment served as an inefficient means of disposing of the subject. He returned, whole and fully healed, several days after his death, joining me in my carriage as our train travelled over the mountains.

I dissembled and queried how this might have happened.

"I do not wish to speak of it," Signore Vashta said, although he showed me the scars where his limbs had been rejoined. They were healing, albeit slowly. Today they are but white marks against the Don Vashta's tanned skin, and one day even those will fade and leave him unblemished.

9.

There are those, upon finding that I travelled with the man, who find my interest in his executions unsavory.

I make no apologies for my friendships.

10.

The most extraordinary aspect of Don Vashta's situation lies the reaction he provokes. He claims to be an evil man, and there are no shortage of crimes attributed to his name, but in truth he is no more evil than many who have suffered the wrath of the law and significantly less evil than most.

Don Vashta is a seductive man, charming in his own way. This is coupled with a streak of cruelty and a thorough disregard for convention, which often sees him accused of an abundance of crimes when others would face a singled charge. That one likes the man, yet loathes themselves for it, is, perhaps, at the heart of the response he evokes from judiciary officials.

11.

When the Government man first came to my house, I asked him a single question. "What is the method of execution?"

The Government Man is short and officious, with a mean haircut and a sallow face. He wears salmon colored shirts that do not suit his complexion. He fidgets and pulls out a handkerchief, coughing into it politely when he realises there's no other reason to have pulled it from his pocket.

"Well," he said, "he's been charged--"

"Not the charges, just the punishment."

I have no use for charges. Now, after all this time, what is one more charge laid at Don Vashta's feet?

"Oh," the Government Man said, and he fidgeted some more. "Well, we wanted your help with that, but we were thinking, maybe...poison?" He peeks at me, furtively, trying to gauge my reaction.

I gave him nothing. "What kind?"

"The...usual kind?"

"Ah," I said, "potassium chloride and all the trimmings. I wish you luck, sir, for his sake and yours."

The government man, more astute than many in his position, raised an eyebrow. "You do not think this will work, sir?"

I assured him I did not. "Signore Vashta has been poisoned before," I said, "with substances far worse than the ones you propose."

When he asked me for options, I ventured, perhaps, a wood-chipper would be in order. Perhaps we should simply fire Don Vashta into space and let the vacuum do its grisly work.

The government man looked at me, as if I might be joking.

If I am honest, dear colleagues, I could not tell you whether I was or was not.

12.

I asked him, once, what the secret was. How he, of all people, returned after every death. We were in a cantina down on the Coast. It had been twenty years since they'd executed him here, and Don Vashta had been overcome with a feeling of nostalgia. When I asked the question he ceased eating his eggs, placed his knife and fork on the table and stared out over the gentle sea.

"At first I thought it was me," he said. "I didn't want to die, so somehow, I simply didn't. Willpower, you know? Or, perhaps, some strange blessing.

"Then the bad days came and I wanted to be punished, but no-one could ever achieve it for longer than a few days. I tried many things and I was planted in the ground, and yet I would return three days later like clockwork, walking into town with no real memory of where I'd been. Those were the worst, Beal. Those years turned me into a monster, and I indulged every whim. A man who cannot die is a man who doesn't fear, and a man who doesn't fear--"

He shrugged and drank his coffee, returned to his eggs.

"These days the deaths are just something that happens. I try not to think about it, and take my pleasures where they come, accepting that one day the inevitable will happen if I but wait my turn."

"Accept?" I said.

"It is better than hope," Don Vashta said. "A man can accept many things, but hope is a knife that digs in his heart until it drives him mad."

13.

Just a few minutes ago, I received the phone call. They are moving Don Vashta by van, transporting him to the site of his seventeenth execution, and they wish me to come along and observe his latest death. A man from the government has been pestering me for days, despite the fact I tell him that I have no interest in such things anymore.

"But you must," the man says, time and again, "He's asked you to be there."

"And I owe Don Vashta nothing, so he has no power to compel my attendance."

"Your government is requesting your presence, sir."

"They," I tell him, "have even less power to compel me than Signore Don Vashta does."

The Government Man says nothing to this. Perhaps he

cannot comprehend it, being free of the government's influence. They have sent him to my house three times in preparation for this day, trying to convince me to do my duty.

"Sir," the Government man says, "I must re-assert that--"

I do not let him finish. "I am not coming, sir," I tell him. "My government can go to hell."

14.

There are those who believe Don Vashta is the devil, and those who believe he is nothing but a hoax, and yet others who are convinced that he has achieved some scientific breakthrough that should be shared with the world.

I have known Don Vashta for many years, have seen him killed thrice and advised on many other deaths, and none of these theories ring true. I can offer you no better explanations, not venture any theories. I was done with such things years ago, and do not wish to return to the habits of a younger self. I do not care to know the mysteries of the world, lest they cease to be mysteries and become drab and plain.

In this, perhaps, I share something with Roland K., who saw a man hung and turned away. I feel, perhaps, a kinship with him, that I haven't felt in a considerably long time.

15.

It should be noted, even today, that Don Vashta remains handsome and young. The stories he can tell you about his various incarcerations, the times he has been locked away or captured by those who experiment on him. He has suffered many forms of punishment and endured them all, knows tricks of escaping prisons and labs that no other man could know.

Don Vashta has a knack for storytelling that I, for my sins, find lacking. Often these stories are brilliantly fantastic and loaded with salacious detail.

This document concerns itself only with Signore Don Vashta's executions, as befits a the records of a man with my interests and experiences.

16.

I am old and I am cantankerous and I fear that my reason is slipping. In truth, I would be at the execution today, but I fear I can no longer perform as needed. My duty to our fraternity has long given way to my duty towards my friend, seeking a means of achieving that which he most desires.

And I fear I bring us into disrepute, despite my best efforts to remain above approach.

The man from the government called me again, asking for clarification on the methods I have suggested. They're going to try them, one after the other, in an effort to rid the earth of the scourge known only as Signore Don Vashta.

He repeated the request that I witness Don Vashta's death, and once again I declined.

17.

It is late. A man from the government waits, in a car, outside my home. He knocked on my door when he first arrived, introduced himself and offered to drive me to the prison. "I know you've said you aren't interested, sir," he told me, "but they wanted me here in case you changed your mind."

I offered him a cup of tea, which he refused. Then he went back to his car and settled into the front seat, reading a magazine by the dim interior light.

The hours advance, merciless as an invading army. I await the phone-call that, inevitably, will come, informing me of the exact time and method of Don Vashta's execution, the various indicators they choose to believe are proof their endeavor has been a success.

I will write details down, for that is the nature of duty. If you are one who has taken an interest, then you live up to the obligations that come with that role. It matters not if you have befriended the man, overlooked his terrible nature and the evil in his past. Duty, it must be said, is duty.

Although even this has limits.

I no longer know which phone-call bothers me more, the inevitable call informing me of his death, or the one that will come later, days after the authorities lose interest in my actions, when a familiar voice will greet me like a co-conspirator and offer a new report.

He will tell me the things he recalls of this death, and the things he recalls of his journey back. There is no joy in this, no mercy in his recollection. It would be easier if I did not answer, but this, too, is duty. And I know that the wait is the worst of it.

It is a long wait, a terrible wait.

At least, for me, there is the knowledge that an end will come.

How unbearable must it be to wake and wake again, to know that one's death is forever out of reach?

18.

Thrice now, in our conversations, he has made me an offer to travel together as we once did. "Beal, old friend," he says to me, "I could use a companion, and there is but one man I trust."

It may be a lie, for I know he's a liar, but thrice now I've elected to deny his offer and remain faithful to my appointed task. Even now, as my fidelity to duty wanes, a part of me longs to keep to the path.

I write this now, from my station here in the Antipodes, and I no longer have the strength to decline his offer if he asks again.

After this, his seventeenth execution, I will acquiesce to Don Vashta's request. I will tender my resignation and be struck from the ledgers, to step away from the pageantry and reason that protects us.

I do this willingly, with full knowledge of what it entails, and know there will be those who cast aspersions on my work once I stray, attempting to refute all I have done in the years before. I accept this also, and choose to go forth regardless.

I will not ask your forgiveness, for I know there can be no such. All I offer is an explanation, and even that a simple one: We forgive a great deal - perhaps too much - of those we already love. And if he asks, I will embrace my friend and pledge myself to travel beside him, watching over his future executions until such time I breath my last.

I do this not to learn his secret, but because all men deserve such, a friend to share their journey and ease the burden of troubles.

If this makes me a monster in the eyes of our fraternity, then I willingly accept the charge.

IT'S NOT A BAD JOB, REALLY

In the end, I go round to Sammi's house. I sit on her couch, picking at the spongy green filling that pokes through the cracked leather. She offers me cigarettes and cups of coffee, content to wait me out. And I make her wait, you know what I'm saying? There are some things you talk about straight away, and some things you hold off and wonder if there's other ways to deal. Maybe, you think. Maybe not. Not talking is always an option, right?

Maybe wins, eventually, 'cause Sammi's house is like that. It's got that feel about it, like you belong there. Like the universe wants you to be there, out on her back deck, surrounded by the ferns and the terra cotta pots. It's the place you're always welcome, even if you don't feel welcome any other place.

And Sammi, she knows when something's up. Sammi always knows. After the third coffee, she says, well, tell me about it, then.

And me, I nod, and this is what I tell her.

.   .   .

It's the afternoon of October nineteen and I'm already tired of work. Phil gets it into his head that we should process the whole damn waiting room before we knock off. It's four o'clock when this goes down, right about the point when we're all getting ready to wind down. Go get a coffee, maybe, or do a little photocopying. Anything we can to eke out a little time away from our desks and the endless clients.

But we all like the job there, one way or another, so we bitch and we moan and we make a few jokes, and we call up the next file and get on with things.

The next file I call up belongs to a wizard. I've never processed a wizard before, but I head to the waiting room and call this guy's name, and he stands and follows me through the office to my cubicle up the back.

He's not what I'm expecting, having looked over his file. This bloke's the kind of big that comes with steroids and weight training. He wears blue jeans and a pale pink button-up shirt he fills out nicely. I could see his scalp through the thin fuzz of hair, but his chin was hidden beneath a pointed goatee. Tattoos on his fingers, loads of 'em. He's got hands as pale as fresh-poured milk and they're covered in blue ink, like he wasn't happy with the lifeline on his palm and figured he could cheat fate by tattooing a new one. Big, thick fingers that seem all soft and unprotected, like the squishy part of a banana once you peel the skin off.

I give him the usual spiel while I look him up on the computer. I get his name, address, place of employment and all that other stuff. I type things into the computer file and it gets syphoned away to the place that stuff goes.

You do not have to provide information willingly, I tell him, but it can make life easier for everyone if he's willing to go along with things. I pour the poor bastard a glass of water and leave it on the edge of my desk. He tells me he's fine to give me what I need. He just wants to get this over with.

Okay, I tell him. Shall we on with it, then?

Yes, he says. Let us.

You understand this interview is the first of several, I tell him. It will still take several weeks for your application to be processed, I tell him.

He wheezes a little, like he isn't sure how to breathe with that muscle packed onto his chest. He waves my statements away with those soft, pale fingers.

I understand, he tells me, and it gave me a queer feeling, Sammi, like he wanted me to be nervous. Like I'd gone in there and crossed some line with him I wasn't supposed to cross.

This guy is all sorts of contradictions I can't quite pin down: soft hands and hard, weight-lifter's muscle. Well-built and wheezing, like his lungs aren't up to the job. Like he was pulling some kind of magic trick that prevented me from seeing what he was really like.

The computers were running slow that day.

He says, your name is Mack. You're wearing the wrong name-tag, yes?

Jesus, Sammi says. I hate it when they try that.

It distracts me when she says it, 'cause she's been all quiet otherwise. And she's thinking this is it, the thing that's been bugging me. I got an asshole weirdo, like you do at the office. Everyone has bad days when the assholes roll in.

He got the name right, I tell her. You've got to give him that one.

You see twenty clients a day, Sami says. You tell them all your name. You think these assholes don't talk to each other? You think they're content with us thinking they're all frauds?

Here's the thing, I tell her. I *was* wearing someone's tag that day. They don't let you out there to interview people without wearing one anymore, and I'd left my tag on the dresser of this guy's bedroom.

Which guy? Sammi says.

This guy. No-one you know.

You haven't said shit about a guy, Sammi says.

It's not a big deal, I tell her. We slept together a couple of times. It's totally not a thing.

Tell me about the guy, Sammi says.

Not yet, I tell her. The guy doesn't matter.

Sammi doesn't look convinced.

What matters, I tell her. What matters is this: I'd borrowed a spare tag from Ali that day, just so I didn't have to listen to another one of Phil's lectures. You remember how those lectures go: blah blah responsibility. Blah blah protocol. So I'm wearing the wrong tag, and this guy got my name. And this wizard guy, he's all: I'm right, yes? You're wearing someone else's name?

And he holds his hand out to me, like I'm going to place the answer right there on his tattooed palm.

They taught us about the cold read during orientation, all the tricks and tactics charlatans use to make it seem like their legitimate. It's all about the non-verbal cues, about asking open questions and letting you hang yourself. They tell you there will be clients who seem like the real deal, clients who can convince you that magic truly exists. I've had clients pull the name-tag thing before, but they didn't do it as smooth as this. They didn't have this guy's conviction. They didn't guess my real name, right off the bat.

There's protocol, when you find yourself wavering like that.

You'll have to excuse me, I tell the client. I need to check a file in the back.

Of course, he says. A file.

He folds those pale hands over his impossibly taut belly and watches me retreat.

Phil comes and finds me in the staff room. He knows what's happened. It's obvious what's happened, when someone pulls a retreat at that point of the afternoon. He's got this look on his face that's not quite concern. Phil doesn't feel concern, not during work hours. He says, you okay? You look kind of pale.

And I'm all, yeah, I'm good. I just caught a live one, you know?

Phil puts his hand on my shoulder and sits down at the table beside me. He doesn't say anything, but he knows what I'm feeling. Of course he knows. He's Phil. He's been doing the job longer than anyone in the office. He's experienced everything: Cabalistic wizards and Enochian sorcerers; witches and psychics and masters of Santería; the weird kids convinced they're mortal avatars for creatures beyond our ken.

Take a moment, Phil says. Get your breath back and keep yourself steady. You know how to handle this. You've been trained, remember?

I hated him, a little, when he said that to me. I know that isn't fair to Phil, but it happened all the same.

. . .

So the Wizard's eyes follow me when I step back into the office. He watches me cross the room and settle down at my desk, watches me take a moment to adjust the stapler and the computer mic that records our interview. I hit the wrong key to activate the mic, so we have to restart after I ask the first question. When I get the recording started, I go back to the beginning and ask him his full name again.

You know my full name, he says. We have already covered this.

I'm sorry. I'm sorry, I tell him. It's the tail end of a very long day.

It is fine, the wizard says. I have practiced the art of patience before. Then he grins and me and takes another wheezing breath. He says, that which we have practiced can be recalled with significant ease, when needed.

I smile at him and he smiles back, confident as anything. We run through the questions on the screen, and he gives me answers that fit the parameters. He says nothing that truly proves he is a wizard. I do not ask him for any direct manifestation of magic, merely ask about where he has lived, where he has trained, whether he is willing to extend his services to the public. All the things the government wants to know, even if they don't believe.

He answers the questions confidently. He knows how to play the game.

He says, you had a pet as a child. A small cat, yes? Black, with a white patch of fur on its forehead.

I stumble over the next question, asking about his annual income from employment outside of magic

You called the cat Alfred, after Batman's butler, he says. You never read the comic books, just watched the TV show. Alfred was hit by a car when you were fifteen, but your parents said he'd run away rather than make you face mortality so early.

I repeat my question over again: what is your estimated annual income, after income from occult or magical methods are excluded.

You have a younger sister, the wizard says. She works in a hospital.

I tell him to stop. I ask him the question about his income a third time, and this time he answers. Quiet. Smug. He has both hands resting on the edge of the desk, one folded into the other.

You do not believe in magic, he says.

No-one does, who works here, I tell him. It's one of the requirements.

He says, And all these things I am telling you, you think they are tricks?

Sure, I tell him. What else can they be?

Magic, he says. The ghosts that hang around you, tangled in your aura.

And that's where he loses me, you know what I'm saying? Every time they pull that trick with ghosts, bringing auras into it. I can almost buy it, when they're doing their mind tricks, but as soon as they start to explain it the whole thing falls apart.

I tell him: mate, I don't believe in auras.

He raises an eyebrow, curious, but does not ask the question.

I tell him: I sure as shit don't believe in ghosts.

Then I sit back in my chair and fold my arms, ignoring the third-last question on the screen. I tell him, three years I've been here, processing clients, and I've never been asked the same question twice. Every one of your fuckers comes in here, trying to prove you're the real deal with all the shit you know. Some of it's right and some of its wrong, but you're always guessing different thing.

If there's shit tangled up in my aura, I tell him, it's

getting free and getting replaced faster than you shits come in.

This is bad protocol. We're not supposed to engage the clients. Not supposed to engage with their crap.

The wizard says, you've never dealt with someone like me, though? You've never handled a full-fledged wizard, just those who make do with the scraps and rags of magic.

Like it matters, I tell him.

It matters, he says.

And I go to tell him it fucking doesn't, but I stop myself at the last minute. He grins at me. He came real close. You're doomed, if you start to argue. You start walking the crooked line away from disbelief. You become the kind of person who believes in magic, and then you'll grant a license. No-one wants that, up in the department. They want us to find reasons to turn people down.

So I ask the last three questions and record his answers on the computer. I print the form and put it in front of him so he can sign the relevant places. I thank him for his time and let him know we'll be in touch. He stands, and once again I remember that he's tall. Tall and well-built, beneath his pink polo shirt.

He wheezes a little, as he stands. How does someone who looks so fit struggle to breathe so hard? And again, I'm contemplating magic. This job will get to you like that.

Thank you, the wizard says. It's been an enlightening afternoon.

He cupped his pale fingers together and raised them to his face. Whispered, quietly, into the pale flesh, and when he pulled his hands apart, he held a grey-furred kitten between his trembling fingers. He offered it to me, and I took it. The kitten mewed at me.

Agency protocol says we're not supposed to accept gifts.

I knew, the moment my fingers made contact, Phil was going to give me hell.

Phil, Sammi says, contempt in her voice. She refills our coffees with the dregs from the plunger, taps a fresh cigarette free of the pack on her coffee table. She settles back in her chair and touches a match to the cigarette, gently breathes against it until the tip glows amber.

He's not that bad, I tell her. He just likes things done a certain way.

I worked there six months, Sammi says. Trust me, he's that bad. The whole place is that bad, once you get out. I bet he marched you down to the pound, made you turn the cat in while he stood there, watching.

He had to do that, I tell her. It's protocol.

Then we sit there and smoke. Take sips from our coffee cups, adding sugar, adding milk. Neither of us says anything until it's time for me to go.

The part of the story I don't tell her is this: I go home with Phil, at the end of the day. We spend the night together, like we've been doing for a while now. I mention the wizard to Phil and he says I shouldn't worry 'bout it. We sit on his couch and he puts his arm around me and he apologies for screaming at me when he found out about the kitten. He reminds me he needs to keep up appearances, 'cause there's protocols against what we're doing, the two of us.

Then he kisses me, on the neck, and he tells me he loves me.

He's not so bad, Phil, when he's like this. When he knows it's just him and me.

I go into the kitchen and get us some beers. Phil likes

his beer from a glass, so I screw the lids off and I pour, beer hitting the side of the glass first so the head doesn't grow too large. I walk them back to the living room and give one to Phil, on the couch. We sit there, drinking quietly, in the glow of the television. I tell him about the wizard, all the stuff he didn't learn when he was giving me hell in the staff room. I don't mention the kitten, from when I was young. I don't mention that at all.

Phil says, I remember the first client I ever had who made me think, yeah, maybe. It was this old guy - a witch doctor - who claimed he could see the spirit of my dead brother hanging around me. He told me he could hear things my brother was saying, messages from the other side and things that only my brother would know. He told me my brother, Steve, was proud of me, and I wanted to believe that so goddamn bad.

He stopped and took a long sip from his beer. His eyes were focused somewhere above the television, not really looking at anything in particular.

I've been there seven years now, Phil says, quietly. I've had all manner of clients try to tell me what Steve's ghost is thinking. It gets easier, over time, once you've started to learn their tactics. But you never stop wishing — just maybe - that they're right. That's how you last in the job, long term. You acknowledge that desire, and you learn how to ignore it.

He finishes his beer and puts the glass on the table without a coaster. I finish mine, not long after. We go to the bedroom and two of us undress. We've been doing this a while now. Long enough that there's no excitement in it, seeing Phil strip out of his clothes, seeing his parts that most people don't get to see. I climb into bed and turn on my side. Phil turns out the lights and crawls in beside me, wraps one arm around my shoulder, presses his belly against my back.

He holds me for a while, whispers in my ear. Eventually I get into it and give him what he wants.

We are sensible people with sensible lives. This is what I think to myself. This is all the magic we need.

I don't tell Sammi any of that.

Phil, she says, eventually, 'cause I've gone quiet. God, she says, Phil. What a goddamn asshole. We need to find you another job. You deserve better than putting up with his shit. I swear, Mack, I swear to god. You're better off getting out of there.

I light another cigarette. Think it over.

It's not such a bad job, I tell her. I think I like it there, really.

THE DRAGONKEEPER'S WIFE

He comes home stinking of sulfur and brimstone, peeling off the leather gloves with black scorch-marks on the fingers and massaging his palms against the laminate counter. His face is peeling, always peeling, the skin baked red and raw by the wyrm.

His wife looks up from her Patricia Cornwell and peers at him through her glasses. She has pale eyes, his wife, as cold and blue as the winter ocean.

"A long day," she says.

"There were protesters," he says. "The noise made it irritable."

He hangs the heavy jacket on the hook by the door, then crosses the room to peck her on the cheek. She turns the page of her novel.

"The dragon's always irritable," she says. "I don't know why you bother."

He shrugs and heads to the bathroom, ready to clean off the stink. Tiny scraps of flesh flake off as he scrubs his face. The new flesh beneath still has the same weary expression the old flesh was wearing.

. . .

There is a ritual to their mornings. Every day starts exactly the same way.

He rubs down raw skin with aloe oil while she makes them both coffee. He eats a bowl of oatmeal while she prepares his lunchbox. He gathers together the parts of his heavy, asbestos uniform while she selects an apple he can eat on the train.

They are vegetarians, both of them, though she would prefer not to be. It's just that you don't want to go near a dragon with meat on your breath, not even the faint whiff left behind by a wife's loving peck on the cheek.

Sometimes, amid the crush of commuters, he wonders what she does with her days. She tells him, of course, but they are just words. There are no details, no physical clues. Her days do not mark her the way the dragon marks him. Her skin is always smooth and pale, her eyes bright behind the thick lens of her glasses. She does not peel, she does not ache.

He bites into his apple, chewing on the cool, woody texture.

"She could be doing anything," he thinks. "Anything at all."

The dragon is snapping at the keepers brushing down its ruby scales. He watches the wyrm for a few minutes. She's right, the dragon is always irritable. But there are shades to her irritation, and time has given him the ability to read them. The dragon is crabby today, prone to snapping, but no-one loses an arm and that's a good sign.

He climbs into his outer uniform and commandeers a brush from one of the other keepers. The wire bristles glow red-hot as they make contact with the dragon. Smoke rises from the leather gloves, fingertips burning as he works the brush in long strokes over dragon scale. He rubs that point, just below the wing, where he knows it likes to be rubbed. The dragon purrs, rumbling like a rock fall, thermal control lapsing as she rakes the wall with her claws.

The keepers back away, stumbling for the doors, baking inside their uniforms as the temperature rises.

He can hear the emergency team outside the chamber, prepping the showers, the fire extinguishers and the ice packs, ready to peel everyone down to blistered skin and red flesh. He stumbles out of the heat and into their embrace. They cool him down and tend his burns, then send the next team in to deal with the dragon.

She is cooking when he gets home: yellow squash and asparagus slavered with garlic and butter, carefully fried over the stove-top. She wears an apron tonight, for the first time in years. He leans against the doorway, his dragon smell fighting with the aroma of fried garlic. She looks up and frowns.

"You're hurt," she says. She puts the wooden spoon on the bench and steps towards him, fingertip reaching out to touch the blisters on his face.

"It's not that bad," he says. His skin stings when she touches him. He should probably take a cold shower. Her nose wrinkles as she breathes in.

"It's wrong," she says. "It's inhumane. It should be stopped."

"The dragon doesn't mind," he says. "It likes having keepers."

She draws her hand back, steps away so she can look

him in the eyes. He grins, the skin cracking at the corner of his lips.

"I wasn't talking about the dragon," she says. She shakes her head and goes back to cooking dinner. He heads towards the shower, rubbing one hand through the stubble of his hair.

It's late, and he's not sleeping. His skin feels stretched and angry. The sheets scratch at him, stinging the raw flesh. He rolls over and shakes her shoulder, waking her up. She looks at him, blinking in the darkness, strange without her glasses.

"What is it?" she says.

"What did you do today?" he says.

"What?"

"What did you do today?" he says. "After I left, before you started cooking dinner. What did you do?"

"Housework," she says. "Some shopping. I think I read a little in the afternoon."

She rolls over and drifts back to sleep. He lies awake, watching her. She is a pale girl, dark-haired and beautiful. He can't remember what it feels like to run his fingers through her hair. His fingers are raw and burned. His lips are cracking at the corners.

He thinks of the dragon, trapped in its room, scales barely containing the bonfire that burns beneath its flesh.

"It's inhumane," he says, mouthing the words carefully, trying the idea on for size. "It's inhumane, it should be stopped."

She does not make coffee the next morning. He eats his

oatmeal in strained silence. She wears a nice dress, green and simple. Her arms are starting to tan.

"What are your plans?" he says. "What's happening today?"

"Housework," she says. "Some shopping. The new Cornwell's out this afternoon. I should go and pick it up."

He takes his apple and leaves, but he doesn't walk to the train station. He simply crosses the road and waits, taking cover behind the trees. He eats his apple slowly, making the sweet tang last as long as he can.

It's a warm day, humid, and his burnt skin stings in the sunlight. It takes three hours for his wife to emerge, her dark hair pulled into a tight bun. She turns left, the wrong direction for the shops, and he watches her walk up the street.

His wife isn't going shopping, but he still goes to work. Three hours late and a different train, the carriages empty now that he's bypassed the rush hour crush. He has to force his way past the protest lines, dozens of picketers waving signs. His pay is docked for being late. He spends the day scrubbing the dragon's scales, paying attention to the taut lines of muscle beneath. His skin gets tighter as the day wears on; he feels almost ready to burst.

"I think my wife lied to me," he says, telling the dragon like the wyrm will understand. "Why would she lie to me?"

There are protestors outside, demanding the dragon's freedom. He resists the urge to explain that the dragon is hot and irritable. Releasing the dragon would be like releasing a forest fire. He pushes through the crowd and walks to the train station.

On the ride home he makes a list. All the reasons he can think of for his wife to start lying, from the obvious to the absurd. It's a short list, stunted, and he wonders if it should be longer.

His skin is peeling again, around the face. The other people in the train carriage stare as he whispers beneath his breath.

She's reading Patricia Cornwell in bed. He hasn't showered well enough to scrub off the stink, so their bed smells like stale egg. She pretends she doesn't notice, licking her finger every time she turns the page.

He stares at her book, wondering if he recognizes the title. Is it the new edition? Did she actually go shopping? He should have paid more attention the other night. He should know these things.

"Honey," he says. "What did you do today?"

His wife rolls over and looks at him, pale eyes peering over the top of her glasses.

"Shopping," she says, and she gestures with the book. "The new Patricia Cornwell, remember?"

He nods. She lays the book down, open, across her chest.

"Since we're asking," she says, "What did you do today? Why does the city keep a dragon in a box?"

He shakes his head.

"I'm not allowed to tell you," he says. "You know I'm not allowed to tell you."

"Sure," she says. She raises her head, looking at him through the glasses, her pupils the size of jellybeans behind the thick lenses. "But that doesn't mean that I'm not allowed to ask."

He is cleaning the dragon's teeth, scrubbing the red-stained maw with a long-handled wire brush. The dragon is snappy today, ready to lash out and take off an arm. He makes soothing noises, low-pitched moans and signs, trying to keep the dragon calm. It works. It almost works. The dragon stops snapping and settles for the occasional nip.

"Is she having an affair?" he asks. "Does she have a part-time job that she doesn't want to tell me about?"

He rinses the brush in a bucket, and the air is filled with steam. The dragon looks pleased when it hears the water hissing. He pulls the brush out, the metal cool and ready. He inserts the brush into the dragon's mouth and resumes the gentle scrubbing. The dragon scowls and hisses.

"I think I'm going to follow her," he says. "Do you think I should follow her? I know it's a breach of trust, but I think I want to know. Should I just ask her? Do you think that would be better?"

The dragon lowers its head and looks at him, eyes full of molten amber. It bares sharp teeth and flicks its split tongue into the air. He reaches out and pets the dragon, scratching behind its ear. It's against the rules to pet the dragon. His glove start smoking, then it starts to burn, but he scratches for as long as he can bear it.

They pull him out of the dragon's chamber and patch up the burns on his hands. His manager yells at him, but there is no punishment. It turns out that petting the dragon isn't actually against the rules. It's just monumentally stupid and they expect people to be smart.

The manager insists that he go see the counselor. He goes along because he wants to keep his job. He tells the counselor about his wife. The counselor listens and says, "I understand," and "Yes, I see." The counselor offers him the number of a registered couple's therapist. The counselor points out that such problems are common between keepers and their wives. The counselor asks him if he has any questions.

He ponders and says, "Why do we keep the dragon? What purpose does it serve?"

The counselor frowns and says, "I'm not allowed to tell you that. You know I'm not allowed to tell you that."

And he says, "Yeah, but that doesn't mean I can't ask. It seems inhumane."

The councilor frowns some more and chews on a pen. Notes are written in a black spiral notebook.

The counselor says, "You appear to be under some stress. I'll organize for you to have a few days off to relax."

He goes home from work two hours early, riding the empty trains with a hand wrapped up in gauze. The sunset is spectacular that evening, full of molten reds and azures that make him think of the dragon's eyes.

When he gets home his wife is out. He wonders where his wife could be. The flat smells like her perfume, sharp and citrus sweet. She hasn't worn perfume for months. He's surprised that he recognizes the smell.

He makes coffee and sits at the table. He waits for his wife to come home.

His wife breezes into the apartment a little after four, her face flushed and pink behind the thick glasses. She carries grocery bags in one hand and a paperback under her arm. She drops the paperback when she sees him, and the bags when she sees the bandages.

"My god," she says, "what's happened to you?"

"I came home early," he says. "There was an incident. Where have you been?"

"Shopping," she says. "I got the new Patricia Cornwell."

He picks up the book. Its cover is plain, but the title is orange and lurid. He rubs the spine with the thumb of his good hand.

"What about yesterday?" he says. "I thought you did that yesterday?"

She rolls her eyes and sits on the other side of the table. She takes the book from him and puts it down on the tabletop.

"I did grocery shopping yesterday, today I got the book."

He looks at the bags of groceries.

"Really?" he says. "Would you really tell me if you didn't?"

His wife looks at him for a long time, her pale eyes shining behind the lens of her glasses. The thumb of the right hand rubs the back of her left wrist. There's a stamp there, green, like the kind they give out at protests. She sighs and blinks, tugging her sleeves down. He tries to picture her there, to see her face among the crowd with their signs and chants.

"No," she says. "I guess you're right. I probably wouldn't."

They lie in bed together, but she's just a weight on the far side of the mattress. He tosses and turns, hand itching beneath the bandages, his wife's eyes haunting him every time he closes his. She has beautiful eyes, pale and blue as arctic ice, but they live behind the glasses now. All he sees are reflections in the thick lenses, his own face staring back where her eyes used to be. His skin is pink and peeling, flaking away in clumps. His hair is singed and stubbled, burned away while patting the dragon. He is missing one eyebrow.

His skin feels taut and tight. He feels like he could break free.

Perhaps he'll quit and follow her, joining the protest mob. Perhaps he'll give up the burn scars, the asbestos uniforms and the life without meat. Perhaps she'll reconsider, staying home and making him coffee. Perhaps they can still be together.

He rubs his good hand across his forehead, wiping away the sweat. She snores a little, wheezing; she's never been a quiet sleeper. His palm is full of peeled skin, fragile as a cobweb. Perhaps there is no perhaps. He has told her everything he knows about the dragon, and tomorrow he will pay for it.

When he closes his eyes, what will happen is this: Tomorrow she will pack her bags and go live with someone else, someone who understands what she means by inhumane. He will sit in the empty apartment, whittling away the hours, waiting until his leave is finished and go back into the dragon's chamber.

Then one day, if he's lucky, their eyes will meet across a protest. He will be a different man then, a man peeled out of the burnt skin of his former self. She will recognize him despite the scars, and her eyes will smile a little with the memory. He will walk over and shake her hand. He will ask about the latest Patricia Cornwell.

Then, if they're very lucky, he will tell her why the dragon is kept in the chamber. He will tell her, and then they'll both be happy.

ON THE FINDING OF PHOTOGRAPHS OF MY FORMER LOVES

I was out when Lisle found the pictures. She was gone by the time I got home.

Leaving was unlike her, but she did it anyway, packing her things and taking off while I was out doing the Saturday afternoon shopping. She'd left me a note on the kitchen table. I sat down to read it, bags of groceries forgotten as I stared at the slip of pink paper with my envelope tucked underneath.

The note was definitely hers. Lisle wasn't the kind of girl for a flowery farewell, but she loved scented notepads and pens shaped like watermelons. She coveted stationary that begged you to lick it and she used it regardless of the circumstances. Her note did its best to smell like a strawberry and it said *Goodbye* in glitter-shot green ink.

The envelope was definitely mine: yellowing and bent from its years behind the filing cabinet, just wide enough to hold a handful of photographs. It smelt like dust and mildew, left stringy threads of spider web attached to the orange tablecloth. When I touched it dust puffed up, dancing in the light filtering in through the curtains. I could feel the solid ridge of the photographs inside and I traced their outline in the dust with a fingertip.

After a while it sunk in: Lisle had left me and I missed her. I put the groceries away and considered that. I hadn't expected to feel anything.

It wasn't until later, when I lay in bed not-sleeping, that it occurred to me to wonder how Lisle had found the envelope. It took some doing to push aside the filing cabinet; it was heavy at the best of times, even before the tax receipts and bank records added their weight to its bulk. I thought it'd been the perfect place to hide my past, all those images and memories I shouldn't have let myself keep. I hadn't moved the cabinet in years myself, not even to dust behind it or chase down the rubber bands that disappeared into the darkness when I got bored at my desk.

Maybe it didn't matter. It still came down to the same thing: Lisle was gone and I'd loved her.

I lay awake trying to figure out how that had come to be.

Photograph One: I took this shot while we were on holidays, three weeks before Christmas in a Disneyland parking lot. Meddy is standing in front of the ticket booth, a tower of black skin against the barrage of pinks, reds and greens. She's well-dressed, as usual; a blend of business casual with comfortable fit. Her jacket was the dark grey of campfire smoke and her snaky locks pulled back, corralled in an undulating ponytail by a black ribbon. It's a good shot, one of the best I've ever taken. The camera loved Meddy's poise, the way she caught good light without trying. She loved being photographed and I loved to capture her on film. Looking through the lens was the only way to stare into her black eyes.

That night, blindfolded, I'd pull the serpents free of their corral. I'd run my tongue along their coarse scales, tasting salt as they writhed beneath my touch. Meddy would pull me back, holding me, running her fingers across my face.

"Careful," she'd whisper. "Careful. I can't control them if they're excited." And I'd run my hand through her hair and let the snakes loop around my fingers, the sensation of muscles tensing as they prepared to constrict. Their tongues tickled the tips of my fingers as they tasted the air. I loved them, the way they felt, the danger of their kiss.

"You'll control them," I'd tell Meddy. "I mean, you love me, don't you?"

I was twenty; she wasn't. It didn't matter at the time.

"I like you," Meddy would tell me. "So do they, well enough. Anything past that and you take your chances. Consider yourself warned."

I took my chance and it didn't work. That hurt for a long time.

Lisle stopped answering her mobile, but she called the land-line three days after her departure. Her voice was sad, over the phone. It cracked as she said hello. "I'm not coming back," she told me. "I just want to get a few things I left behind."

"I'll be gone Tuesday evening," I said. "You come can take whatever you want then."

I wrote the date on the kitchen calendar with a thick, black-ink pen. It was Lisle's calendar, really. She'd decorated it herself. Tuesday's square was filled with stickers, little rainbows and black cats.

"Make sure you're out," Lisle said. "I don't want to see you."

I told her I would and I hung up the phone. I scratched at Tuesday's stickers with my thumb and peeled them off, one by one.

When Tuesday night came round I was sitting on the front step, waiting to Lisle to arrive. She showed up in someone else's car, an old Safari van I didn't recognize. Gave me a sad look when she saw me, like she knew a fight was coming. I hadn't shaved since she left me and still she hadn't changed her mind.

"A Safari?" I said. I was dressed to leave, ready to play my part. I stared at the van, trying to work out where it'd come from.

"You're supposed to be out," Lisle said. "You said you were going to be out."

"I'm running late," I told her. I made a show of lacing my right sneaker, sneaking quick peeks at the driveway.

"Well?" Lisle said. She waited, rubbing one eye. When I didn't move she sniffed a little, put her hand on her hip and glared. I started lacing my other sneaker, taking my time.

Lisle said, "Are you going or what?"

I shook my head and tried to smile. "Come out for a beer," I said. "Let's talk about this."

"No beer," she said, and sighed. "I just came for my stuff, okay?"

I stood up. I looked at her. Her eyes were bloodshot beneath her glasses.

"Just a beer," I said. "You and me, we can talk things out. Or not, if you'd prefer. Just come have a drink and a game of pool, we can catch up and I can apologize."

Lisle shook her head and looked away. She had a blunt face when you saw it in profile. Freckles and glasses, a flat nose she'd hated since childhood. She thought herself awkward but I didn't agree. Lisle sent like soap and laughed like she meant it. I wanted to touch her, to brush her check. I clenched my fist and resisted.

"Come for a beer," I said. "One beer. Who could it hurt?"

"No." Lisle took a deep breath, forced herself to meet my stare. "There's nothing to talk about. I'm leaving, Deacon. You've just got to deal with that."

Then she turned around and left, disappearing into the Safari and keying the ignition. It coughed twice, spluttering to life when she put it in reverse. I watched her go. I took a deep breath. The Safari disappeared down the street.

Someone once told me that marriage is a process of compromise, a little bit of give and take. Lisle and I were good at that, once upon a time, before the ceremony and the dress. She was curious about the past, of course, everyone is in the beginning. She even asked about the others once, brought it up while we were driving home after a movie.

"Does it matter?" I said. "The women I've dated, the good and the bad, they led me to you. That's enough, right?"

Lisle nodded and bit her lip. The answer didn't make her happy, but it seemed like she was satisfied. We didn't talk about it again, not for a long time, but we had an understanding. I'd lived a full life before we met and so had she. That kind of thing is a given these days. Everyone has a past and you do your best to pretend it doesn't matter. Digging up history only leads to trouble.

We'd been dating for three years when I asked her to marry me. No-one was surprised when Lisle said yes.

Friends took us out to celebrate and let Lisle show of the ring. She picked a karaoke bar and we sang Endless Love, Lisle flashing her left hand at the stage lights as we warbled off-key. We were drunk and we were terrible, but people cheered us anyway. No-one could miss the ring, or the way we'd make out in the corner before we started the song. We were young, in love and happy. You couldn't ask for more than that.

The Karaoke finished at midnight and everyone went home. Lisle and I were lying in bed and she asked me the second time. "Who was there, before me? I'm wearing the ring now, you've got me for good. Don't I deserve to know?"

"No," I said. "It's not a good idea."

Lisle pouted, then she kissed me. She ran her fingers down my back. "Tell me," she said. "Tell me about them. Who did you love before I came along?"

And the third time she asked I told her, because there's rules about things like that. I told her about all of them, and then I held her as she cried.

Photograph Two: I took this photo in her workshop, catching Ari at her loom. She's focused on her weaving, legs dancing among the threads. She was all pale silk skin and ridges of black chitin; curves like an hourglass and red facets to her eyes. We'd met at a craft fair two weeks earlier, Ari slipping me her card while my girlfriend haggled about price.

"Come see me without her," Ari told me, whispering in my ear. "We can keep things clandestine."

Ari's lips tasted like poison, acrid and smoky on the tongue. I loved the feel of her chitin under my fingertips, the way she'd cage me with her spider legs and pin me down during the night. Her voice was soft and dark; a song-song lilt that that soothed me while I slept. She made me forget about the guilt that marked our nights together.

In bed Ari's legs would brush my back, all feather-light ecstasy. I would kiss her curves and her as she spun webs and tied me down. I loved her. I thought I loved her. Sometimes I think of my girlfriend and sigh.

"I'm leaving her," I'd tell Ari. "I love you. This isn't fair to anyone."

I was twenty-three; Ari wasn't. I should have known better this time.

"You don't love me," Ari said. "You're here because I want you to be, anything else is just a lie."

I lied to myself for a long time. The knots took longer to untie.

～

I walked into our bedroom the week before the wedding and found Lisle crying, curled up in a tight ball with wet cheeks and puffy eyes. I sat down on the bed and waited. Lisle sniffled and did her best to smile. "I want to love you," she said. "I want to love you so much."

Then she sniffled and a tear leaked out. I leaned over and touched it, kissed it off my finger with a smile. I kissed her cheeks, then her eyes, then her cheeks a second time. "What's wrong?" I said and Lisle sniffled again. She sat up, rubbing an arm across her eyes.

"I want you to be mine," she said. "Really mine."

I hugged her and she nestled under my right arm, held me tight with her spindly arms. "Then I'm yours," I said. "Heart and soul, until the end of time."

"But you're not," Lisle said. "You can't just say it. All

those girls, Deacon. All those other girls. How can you love me after them?"

And that time I didn't say anything. I kissed her and waited, she stroked the edge of my elbow with her right hand; my shirt grew damp from her crying.

"What can I do?" I said. "What do you need me to do? What will make you happy?"

Lisle looked up. It's the first time I'd seen her without glasses, the first time I remembered anyway. Her eyes were blue and bright. "If I had one wish," she said, "just one, I'd wish that you'd never dated any other girls before you met me. I wish I didn't have to share you, not even with their memories."

"Then I won't," I said, and I meant it. I loved her, I really did. It didn't seem a big thing to ask at the time.

So that weekend we exorcised them, all my former loves.

We tossed out the books they'd inscribed and the furniture I'd inherited, all the teddy-bears and the knick-knacks that infested my wardrobe. I stopped using the recipes they'd taught me and stopped visiting the restaurants we'd discovered together. I forgot all the moments I might remember with fondness, all the happy memories and the bittersweet ones that followed. I gave them up, wiped away their fingerprints, and I scoured off the permanent marks they'd left behind.

The only things I kept were the photographs, hidden behind the filing cabinet. A handful of memories shoved into an envelope and left somewhere secret in case I needed them. Then I forgot the envelope as best I could, until Lisle found it and left it on the kitchen table to explain why she walked out of my life.

Lisle came and collected the last of her things under the cover of daylight, raiding the house while I was at work and leaving her key in the letterbox. I came home and spent a few minutes pacing through the house, feeling out the empty spaces where things used to be.

The television was gone, along with one of our couches. She'd taken the coffee pot and the vase with a puppy painted on it. I still had our bed, but she'd taken all the pillows. The envelope and the photographs were still sitting on the kitchen table, half-spread out like she'd gone through them and then changed her mind. I gathered them up and straightened them into a neat pile, wondering how far she'd gotten before she was sorry that she'd looked.

Lisle had left me her wedding ring and a number scrawled on pink paper. I waited a few days before calling her, shuffling through the photographs to fill the time. I'd forgotten so much, but I remembered them now. I remembered those girls and it made my mouth turn dry.

Photograph Three: I took this in my bedroom, that first morning I'd lured her there. Phix curled up on the bed, a paw across her nose. The black hair on her head glossy and lush in the daylight, her wings curled up tight around her like a quilt. Her fur is tawny and sleek, a lion in repose. Her soft purr would have echoed through the room, a noise like distant thunder. Soon she'd wake up and stretch, and I'd admire the arc of her back.

She'd see me with the camera and she'd pounce on me in an angry whirl. Phix had this weird thing about photographs; she loved posing for them but she hated the click of the camera. Catching her off-guard was a challenge, but I did with this picture, snapped off on that first morning when she'd stayed the long night.

I'd met her on the Internet, chatting via e-mail. We used riddles as foreplay, running through the same conversation every time: Four legs, two legs, three legs. Who am I?

"The riddle," Phix would whisper. "I want you to answer."

I'd ask her what would happen if I got the answer wrong.

"Then I'll strangle you," Phix would purr, and she'd give me a wicked smile. "But you'll like it, I promise. I know what I'm doing."

And I'd answer her, incorrectly, to move onto the good stuff. We both knew the answer was man, but she never seemed to mind. "I love you," I told her, and she'd wrap her hands around my throat.

I was twenty-nine, she wasn't. It seemed normal this time.

"I love you too," she told me. We were happy for a while.

~

The phone rang three times before Lisle answered. I didn't recognize the number.

"It's about time," she said. "It's been four days Deacon, you should have called earlier." And when I closed my eyes I could see her saying it, the soft twist and hard lines of her sneering lips and scowl.

"If you were here, right here, I'd kiss you right now," I said. "I'd kiss you and you'd taste like a slice of ripe mango. You'd smell like soap, like you've just climbed out of the shower. I miss the way you smell, Lisle. I'd kiss you because I miss you."

"Stop it," she said. "Christ, Deacon."

"Come home," I said. "Tell me it's not over. I'll destroy the photographs. I'll do it properly this time."

I remember the pause then, the moment when she considered the offer. I remember opening my eyes and looking around our living room, the empty spaces where the couch used to be, the stale-cheese on the pizza boxes that had been piling up where the television had been. I remember holding the envelope in my hand, all the photographs inside.

"It's not enough," Lisle said. "It's more than the photographs, Deak. It's always been more than that. You were distant. Distant and sad. I couldn't deal with that anymore."

I told her I loved her. I think I believed it, but she didn't believe me, not this time.

"Why me?" Lisle said. "After all that, what led you to me?"

"You were ordinary," I told her. "I needed that, I think, after…"

I didn't say it. She said it for me.

"All those girls?" she said. "Christ, those girls, Deacon, they were monsters."

I shrugged, though she couldn't see it. I spread the photographs out on the couch, arranging them in a pile. "We always love the monsters after they've broken our heart."

"I'm not a monster," Lisle whispered. "Not even close. I was good to you, Deacon."

She was, but I didn't say it. And sometimes she wasn't, but I didn't say that either. Neither of us said anything for a really long time. Then Lisle said goodbye and hung up her phone. I held my phone to my ear and listened to the dial-tone change, wishing I had a photograph of Lisle to add to the pile.

THE CLOCKWORK GOAT AND
THE SMOKESTACK MAGUS

Attend—in the darkest streets of Unden there lay a coal-filled fen known as Moloch Alley, a place filled with men who possessed souls with the consistency of smoke, stained and dirty, willing to drift with the whims of the wind and disappear, puff, when the storm winds whistled between the looming factories. A cold place, and a mean one, the air thick with black smoke and men cursed with black lungs and wicked coughs and few hopes for the future. And into this alley walked a clockwork goat, trip-trapping, tick-tocking, marching stiff-legged and determined down the soot-stained cobblestones. It walked into the darkness until it arrived at the copper door of the Smokestack Magus' home, a portal laid flush with the bellowing redbrick chimney of a smelting house, as though one could walk through it and into the roaring furnace beyond.

There were stories, even then, that spoke of the door and its owner. The door was never hot, not even warm, no matter how much smoke billowed forth from the tip of the smokestack, and there were sigils carved into its surface with a delicate hand. The stories said that the only visitors to whom the Magus' door opened were exotic creatures and mysteries. There had been a hippogriff once, or so it was said, not three years prior— a sleek beast with grey-black feathers and sharp teeth used for rending flesh. Before that there had been a marsh troll, and there were stories, older still, about a mermaid, scaled and beautiful, who had been wheeled along the alley's cobblestones in a great tank of brackish water pushed by her small flotilla of slaves, who had knocked and gained admittance but failed to emerge after that.

And now there was the clockwork goat, a device no more than three feet tall with ticking parts of silver. Not even a living thing, not quite, but it looked close enough and there are stories about goats, even here, far from the fireside tales of their childhood, and thus no-one molested the small creature, allowing it to approach the Magus' door without harm when any normal man would fear for his life in the dark shadows of Moloch Alley.

The goat marched up to the door and knocked with one hoof, rapping it against the burnished copper, before settling on its haunches in a flurry of sharp clicks and grinding gears. For three days the goat waited there, sitting on the doorstep while Moloch Alley filled with smoke and dust and ashes, and every day, on the last bell of the thirteenth hour, the clockwork goat would rise and knock and settle on its haunches once more.

It was not until the fourth day that the copper door swung open, magically, before the sharp rat-a-tat of the goat's knock. The goat stood, watching the darkness, until the Magus appeared through the smoke and studied his visitor. He was a short man, black-robed, with eyes like polished coal, and he watched the goat with suspicion on his face. "So," he said, stroking his beard of glowing